CW00867755

The Adventures of Bluedoe

Written by Kristen Byrer
Illustrated by Jon Byrer

Kristen Byrer (signature)
Jon Byrer (signature)

This book is dedicated to my Husband who never stops. And my Dad who never stops reading.

Up north there lives a dog named, Bluedoe.
He lives where the land is both high and low.

On a hill, above the Long Swamp is home for Blue.
He has many friends, but you can visit him too.

Bluedoe is a tiny hound.
His eyes are huge, brown, and round.
He has two ears both long and black.
They reach all the way down his back.

He has a very special nose.
It follows the scent wherever he goes.
Like many puppies he has big paws,
and the cutest little puppy claws.

Blue loves to go on an adventure or exploration
where he learns about the world
and uses his imagination.

Each day he ventures from the cozy house
to say hello to his friend, Cheese, the mouse.

Cheese lives in a burrow in the rock wall.
So Bluedoe imagines that he is very small.

"How are you this morning, Cheese?"
    Asks the dog.
"I'm good. I just saw our friend, Mr. Frog."

Mr. Frog is heading down to the Long Swamp
and his favorite swimming hole.

You know the spot, I'm sure.
It's got mud, rocks, and sticks galore."
"Of course!" says Blue.
"Bye, Cheese! Yahoo!"

Bluedoe pretends he is a frog,
instead of a tiny hound dog.
He hops and leaps, and jumps along the trail.
He stops for a moment to chase his tail.

He listens and hears a "rib-bit" sound.
Bluedoe runs down and he sniffs the ground.
It sounds and smells just like a frog.
He must have just jumped in the bog!

Bluedoe notices a beautiful rock in the sun.
He thinks it would be delicious to chew. Such fun!

He walks a bit closer to give it a lick,
But as soon as he does, the rock gives a kick.
"Ouch!" Yelps the pup, "what could that be?"
"Excuse me pup, you can't chew me."

From the opposite side, on the other end,
Bluedoe sees the face of a familiar friend.
"Sorry Speedy," exclaims the hound!
"You blend in with these rocks all around."

"It's alright," says the turtle, Speedy.
"My shell is the best protection for me."

Blue pretends he has a rock on his back
to protect him from all kinds of attack.

Bluedoe listens with his big floppy ears.
Something amazing is just what he hears.

Plop! Splash! The river loud and alive
with fish, frogs, and turtles that swim and dive.
The puppy sees an animal long and sleek.
She lives in the river and gives Blue a peek.

The fish blows a bunch of bubbles.
"What are those?" the puppy puzzles.

"Bubbles happen when air meets water,
that's how and why.
You can do it puppy, come on and give it a try."

Bluedoe imagines he's a fish and gives a blow,
sticks his nose in the water
and let's some air flow.
Bubbles burst up right out of the water!
"That was perfect," says the fish,
"but swimming is harder."

"I'll imagine swimming for now,
see you next time."
Bluedoe runs along the river
blowing bubbles in his mind.

Soon he hears another sound from the sky.
This animal has wings and can fly really high.
It sings music up in the air.
Wow! This bluebird must be quite rare.

"That's cool! I can sing too,
Just listen to what I can do."
He strolls along
And sings a song...

"Blue is my favorite color.
There can be no other
Quite like Blue!
It's the shade of the sky
And blueberry pie.
Its true!"

"Oh my," chirped the bluebird.
"I can't believe what I've just heard.
This puppy has a sweet musical howl!
That was so nice, please, pup, give us a bow."

As his friend flies off to sing the new blue song,
Bluedoe realizes that something is wrong!
The light is fading and it's getting dark.
"I must run home," the pup cries with a bark!

"My family is waiting for me to come in.
 They will be worried about where I have been."
He smells the path back, the way he has come.

"I'll go back exactly the way I came from!
I can always follow my trail back to my home.
My nose knows the way no matter where I roam."

He runs back past the river, to the Long Swamp
only this time it's not a lazy romp.

He hurries by his frog and turtle friends
over to the spot where the long swamp ends.
He climbs the path up to the house on the hill;
where a warm fire will take away any chill.

He tries to explain what he saw and pretended,
but he is so tired from the energy he expended.
The fire is so cozy.
His eyelids are so heavy.

All the day's adventures race through his head,
but now it's time for Blue to go to bed.
He falls asleep in his most favorite space
with his family near the fireplace.

He will have adventures again.
Tomorrow, he can play pretend.

But, for now, its nighty-night.

The End

Made in the USA
Middletown, DE
18 May 2015